Lady Rample and the Haunted Manor

Lady Rample Mysteries – Book Eight

Shéa MacLeod

Shéa MacLeod

Lady Rample and the Haunted Manor
Lady Rample Mysteries – Book Eight
COPYRIGHT © 2019 by Shéa MacLeod
All rights reserved.
Printed in the United States of America.

Cover Art by Amanda Kelsey of Razzle Dazzle Designs
Editing by Alin Silverwood

The characters and events portrayed in this book are fictitious. Any similarity to real persons, living or dead, is coincidental and not intended by the author.

Chapter 1

The very last thing I expected to find on my doorstep that gloomy autumn morning in October of 1933 was Lola Burns.

I'd been after the milk since my maid, Maddie, had a head cold and was laid up in bed, and I was desperate for tea. But when I swung open the door, there she was—Lola, not Maddie—looking just as blonde and fabulous as she had in Los Angeles.

I'd met Lola several months ago at her wedding to one of my Aunt Butty's old friends. The poor man had promptly been murdered, and I'd found myself involved in the investigation. Something that was becoming an unfortunate habit of mine. Last I knew, Lola had taken up with her dashing young chauffeur, Sam.

She is, you see, an American film star. So naturally I'd never dreamed I'd find her standing on the stoop of my London townhouse, draped theatrically in a mink stole with a dramatic little red felt slouch hat pulled low over one eye.

She tossed her golden locks and said, "Well, ain'tcha gonna ask me in?"

Lola may be an American movie star, but most of the time she sounds more like an American gun-moll. I half expected Al Capone to jump out of the shrubbery.

"Er, yes. Come in, Lola. Nice to see you," I said in that properly pleasant way that had been drilled into me since birth.

Lola stepped into my foyer which was a neat little room edged on one side by a rather lovely staircase. There was lots of elegantly carved crown molding, a heavy crystal chandelier, and highly polished wood floors covered over in expensive Aubusson rugs. A neat little marble and mahogany Art Deco table held a vase of pink hot-house roses.

"Ain't this fancy," Lola said, peering around. "Must be nice, being a lady and all."

My name is Ophelia, Lady Rample, and while I wasn't born into wealth or a particularly high status, I married rather well. When my husband, Felix, left me for the great port and cigar party in the sky, he bequeathed me this townhouse, along with a property in France, and all his worldly goods save his title and a crumbling manor in the wilds of Yorkshire. Those had gone to his cousin, Binky. Binky still hasn't forgiven me. I lose a great deal of sleep over it. That was sarcasm, for the uninitiated.

"Yes, it is, rather," I said. "May I take your stole? How about a drink?"

"Yes, please!" She tossed her stole at me and strode in the direction of the kitchen.

"Ah, this way, Lola," I said, pointing toward the sitting room. "What will you have?" I asked once she was seated on my sofa next to a low burning fire. The sitting room was one of my favorite places in the house with its marble mantlepiece and peacock blue walls.

"G & T, doll. The kids got me hooked."

I was also not best pleased to be forced to mix the drinks myself. Maddie was much better at it.

"Kids?" I asked, whipping up a gin and tonic for her and a highball for me. I much prefer whiskey over gin, though I will drink what's available, if I must.

"Sure. I'm here in London doing a film over at Lime Grove, see?"

"Oh, I see." I guess that explained what she was doing in London. Lime Grove was a movie studio. I handed her the G & T and then took a seat in one of the comfortable armchairs. "Have you been here long?"

"Couple of weeks. I'll be here up 'til Christmas, probably." She took a long swallow of her drink.

"That's... lovely," I said, not sure what else there was to say. "Is it a nice film?"

"Some period piece. Swords and corsets. You know the drill."

I honestly had no idea, but I nodded sagely. "Are you and Sam still an item?"

She snorted. "He's cute and all, but I can do better. Got my eye out for a Viscount or somethin'. So when they offered me this gig, I hopped a boat to England fast as I could."

"And you thought you'd stop by for a visit."

"Well, that and I need your help."

It was my turn to take a long swallow of my drink. "*My* help? Whatever for?"

She leaned forward. "I want to get in good with these people, see?"

"I see." I assumed she meant the movie people.

"I thought I could throw a little party. For Halloween, you know. It's just around the corner. I figured you know lots of people. You could help." She beamed as if I would naturally be thrilled to put my life on hold and plan a party for her.

"Ah. You mean, you thought that me having a title would impress your fellow thespians."

Her brow wrinkled. "I ain't one of those. I like men."

I blinked. "Actors, Lola. Your fellow actors."

Her brow unwrinkled and she laughed. "Yeah! I'd love to show those bozos a thing or two. They think I'm some lame duck American. Well, they'll see. I know swanky folks, too."

I opened my mouth, about to tell her in no uncertain terms that I did not have time to plan a party, nor did I wish to play her show pony, when the front door crashed open. We both started.

"Ophelia!" Aunt Butty shouted. "You'll never guess who's in town!"

Lola and I both relaxed as the door banged shut and footsteps echoed along the hall. Aunt Butty appeared in the doorway, mouth rounded as she caught sight of Lola.

My aunt is sixty-something, ridiculously wealthy, utterly bohemian, and inordinately fond of flamboyant hats. Today's offering was a sort of stiff beret in a nice claret color. One side of the beret dipped low along her head, while the other stood at proud attention a good foot or so in the air. From it dripped a lot of orange fringe which swayed with her every move. It was mesmerizing.

"New hat, Aunt Butty?" I said.

"Indeed." She preened. "Maurice has outdone himself. And I see you've discovered my news. None other than Lola Burns herself has graced London with her presence! Welcome, Lola." And she bent over to give Lola cheek kisses, nearly smothering her in her ample bosom in the process.

"Lola's asked with help planning a Halloween party," I said. "I told her—"

"What a marvelous idea!" Aunt Butty clapped her hands. "We shall commence planning immediately. Get me a drink, Ophelia. And make it a double!"

As I got up to mix my aunt a drink, I said, "But we haven't anywhere to hold such a party. My place certainly isn't big enough, and neither is yours."

"I know the perfect place," she said. She turned to Lola. "Vesseden Abbey. It's meant to be haunted."

Lola clapped, expression ecstatic. "It sounds like the bee's knees!"

"Oh, it's perfect," I said dryly, "If you don't mind being half strangled by cobwebs. The place has been deserted for ages." I handed Aunt Butty a highball and refreshed Lola's G & T. "We haven't time to clean the place."

"Who needs cleaning," Lola said. "You can't buy that kinda staging."

I supposed she was right. "Very well. Who shall we invite to this shindig?"

As Lola and Aunt Butty made lists of invitees and menus and ideas for entertainment, I made my own list. At the very top was a bucket of salt. Any ghost who tried to haunt me was going to have another think coming.

Shéa MacLeod

Chapter 2

Vessenden Abbey loomed out of the fog, a ghostly apparition of Gothic architecture with arched windows and the occasional spire poking from the mist. From what I'd read, the original monastery had burned down centuries ago, but when the place was rebuilt by the Vessenden family, the remains had been incorporated into the building. Hence the name Vessenden Abbey.

Rumor had it the place was inhabited by a multitude of ghosts. I just hoped none of them bothered me while we were here.

I passed the dilapidated gatehouse, pulled around the circular drive, and parked close to the front door. Maddie—

who'd finally gotten over her cold—let out a sigh of relief from the backseat. She hated driving almost as much as my aunt did.

Hale Davis, my paramour for lack of a better term, chuckled beside me. "Don't get too excited, Maddie. Look where she's dragged us."

"If I get dragged to the portals of Hell, I'm haunting you forever, my lady," Maddie said tartly.

"Fair enough," I said.

We all climbed from the vehicle in time to see Aunt Butty's Bentley sweeping up the drive, Simon, her chauffeur, behind the wheel, and next to him Mr. Singh, her Sikh butler with Flora her maid crammed between them. Behind the Bentley came my best friend, Chaz Raynott, with Lola in his roadster. No doubt she'd spent the trip trying to work her charms on him to no avail. Lola wasn't his type. In fact, there wasn't a *woman* on Earth who was his type. But of course that was a thing we kept close to the vest, so to speak, which is why he often squired me about when Hale was busy with his band.

Hale joined me as I stared up at the gloomy monstrosity. Numerous windows stared like blank eyes out onto a grim landscape of barren trees. Leaden skies promised rain soon, and cold wind whipped around the corners of the building, howling like tortured souls of the damned. I shivered and told myself not to let my imagination run wild.

Hale wrapped his arm around him, his eyes twinkling. He knew exactly what I was thinking. "It's just an old house, my love. Don't let it get ya down."

I reached up to press a kiss to his freshly shaven jaw. His dark skin was smooth beneath my lips, and he turned his head to give me a proper kiss.

Hale was an American jazz musician, and we'd met several months ago over a dead body. More or less.

"Well, ain't this a marvel," Lola said, staring up at the manor house as Aunt Butty joined us. "There must be a million ghosts in there."

"One on the grounds and at least three inside," Aunt Butty assured her. Today my aunt wore a turban of purple and gold silk with a cluster of wax grapes artfully spilling from it. Probably she thought it would be fitting for the occasion.

She marched straight up to the door, skeleton key in hand. She'd been the one to let the place for the party, so I supposed it was only fitting she go first. Just in case the ghosts got irritable.

While Mr. Singh, Simon, Maddie, and Flora brought in the luggage, we inspected the digs. On the ground floor was a large dining room to the right and the library to the left. Beyond the entrance hall was the sitting room, a billiards room, and a morning room, next to the kitchen and butler's pantry.

Someone had aired out a few of the bedrooms and living areas so they'd be habitable, but most of the furniture was still draped in spooky white dustcovers and the foyer, at Aunt Butty's instruction, had been left festooned with cobwebs and dust. It was, in a word, atmospheric.

"The perfect setting for a Halloween soiree, don't you agree?" Aunt Butty said, not waiting for an answer. She threw open the doors to the sitting room, which was stuffed to the gills with heavy, dark furniture. "Marvelous. What do you think, Lola?"

"This place gives me the heebie jeebies." Lola shivered.

Aunt Butty grinned. "Perfect."

I wasn't sure what woke me, but I was suddenly sitting bolt upright in bed, blinking in the darkness. My head felt muzzy and my tongue thick and pasty. Aunt Butty had been trying various "Halloween inspired" cocktails on us in an attempt to find the right drink for the party. We'd all gone to bed more than a little tipsy.

Not hearing anything but the wind howling around the manor and Hale snoring softly beside me, I sank back down onto my pillow. Hale cuddled closer, murmuring something in his sleep. I must have been dreaming.

A blood curdling scream echoed down the hall.

This time we both sat bolt upright. Hale snapped on the light. His dark eyes were alert.

"What was that?" I demanded.

"Dunno." He was already out of bed, shrugging into his robe. "Definitely a woman."

I suddenly feared my aunt or Maddie was in trouble. Rolling out of bed, I grabbed my own robe and followed him out the door.

We found Lola at the top of the stairs, staring down like she'd seen a ghost. Her face, already pale, was dead white, and her unpainted mouth made a wide "oh."

"What is it, Lola?" I demanded. "What's wrong?"

Her mouth opened and closed like a fish, but no sound came out.

"What the devil?" Chaz shouted from down the hall.

"Is someone dead?" Aunt Butty arrived with curlers in her hair and her bathrobe askew.

Meanwhile there was thumping somewhere at the back of the house. A door was flung open and Mr. Singh arrived, Maddie and Flora hot on his heels. The only one that wasn't there was Simon who was staying in the old chauffeur's quarters in the garage and was probably blissfully asleep.

Everyone yammered at once... "What happened?" "I heard a scream!" "Is everything alright?" Did someone break-in?" "I need my beauty sleep, you know."

That last one was from Chaz.

Hale held up his hands and managed to shush everyone. "Now, Lola," he said, taking her gently by the upper arms, "tell us what happened? Why did you scream?"

Lola pointed down the stairs toward the foyer. "Sh-she was th-there. I-I s-saw her." Her teeth chattered, though I didn't think it was from the cold, despite her rather gauzy peignoir.

"Who was there?" I demanded. I'd forgotten to put on slippers and my feet were near frozen.

She blinked. "I-I dunno." Her voice had taken on the full gun-moll inflections she usually tried hard to hide. She pointed left to right. "She walked from there to there, dressed like she was right outta *Gone with The Wind* or somethin'. Almost had a heart attack."

"Who was it?" Mr. Singh demanded. He took his job of protecting my aunt very seriously.

"I dunno," Lola wailed.

A stranger in the house wandering around in the middle of the night? That was dashed odd, if you asked me. "What was she doing?"

"Carrying a vase of flowers."

"In the middle of the night?" Aunt Butty said.

"Never mind the middle of the night," Hale said. "What was she doing here at all? There's not supposed to be anyone here but us, right?"

"Correct," I said. "And whoever she is, she isn't one of us."

"That's for sure." Lola said, finally coming around. "I could see right through her."

We all stared at her.

Finally, I asked, "What do you mean, you could see through her?"

"Well, duh, she was a ghost."

Chapter 3

We all slept in a bit the next morning thanks to our late-night adventures. By the time I arose, Hale was already gone, no doubt to explore the grounds. I dressed quickly in a simple gray wool dress and threw a brightly colored cream-and-blue-embroidered cashmere kimono over it to ward off the chill of the old building.

I found Chaz and Lola in the dining room, surrounded by piles of pumpkins. I stared for a moment, unable to come up with a reason there would be pumpkins at breakfast. Finally, I gave up.

"What the deuce?" I helped myself to a cup of tea from the tarnished silver urn on the sideboard.

"Lola insisted," Chaz said.

"We've got to make jack-o-lanterns," she informed me.

"Aren't those made out of gourds or turnips or something?" I'd read about the practice and the folklore in some book or other.

"In America we carve them out of pumpkins. Ain't Halloween without 'em," Lola informed me.

"Aren't pumpkins pig food?" I said.

She gasped in horror. "Why would you feed 'em to the pigs? What a waste when you can make pie out of 'em."

The idea of pumpkin pie was beyond me, but I supposed if she wanted to carve them up for Halloween, she could go right ahead. This was her party, after all.

Unfortunately, what I hadn't realized was that she planned on me helping her. I am not, however, one to dive into something messy myself when I can delegate, and so Maddie found herself, carving knife in hand, scraping out the innards of several of the orange squashes and carving faces into them while I stood by, armed with tea, offering my advice.

"That looks dreadful," I told her as she stabbed wildly at her pumpkin. "It looks like it could use a prune or two."

"It's meant to be spooky, my lady." Her expression was peeved.

Lola assured us the spookier the better.

"Speaking of spooky," I said as Maddie gave our pumpkin leering eyebrows, "have you recovered from last night, Lola?"

"I think so." She looked a bit embarrassed. "I know it's silly, but weird things have been happening lately. I'm not getting a lot of sleep."

"Weird how?" I asked.

"Well," she dug a hole into orange pumpkin flesh, widening it into a gaping maw, "ever since I arrived in England, I've been getting all these mysterious deliveries."

Maddie looked curious but pretended to focus on her squash.

"What do you mean?" I prodded.

"Well, the night I arrived, there was a flower delivery to my hotel room."

"That's nice," I murmured. "No doubt your director or producer welcoming you."

"You'd think, right? But there was no note, and when I asked around, no one knew anything about it." She gouged another hole in the pumpkin, and I winced at the viciousness.

"I wouldn't have thought anything of it, exceptin' the next day I got a note sayin' how did I like the flowers."

"That doesn't seem particularly strange," I pointed out.

"Does when it's signed Cyril."

Maddie's eyes widened.

I blinked. "As in your husband?" Or rather, former husband. Cyril Brumble had been married to Lola for all of five minutes before he'd been murdered.

"Yup. Gave me a turn, I can tell you." Another stab at the poor squash. "Thought maybe it was a joke or somethin'."

"If it was, it was in poor taste," I said tartly.

"You got that right. But then I started gettin' these phone calls. No voice or nuthin'. They'd just hang up. And then sometimes there'd been this sort of spooky sound in the background, like ghosts howling. Like maybe I was gettin' a call from beyond the grave." She shivered.

Maddie snorted. I shot her a look which she ignored, as usual.

"Nonsense," I said stoutly, but a chill went down my spine. "No such thing."

"How do you explain it then?" Lola gave her pumpkin a critical once-over before setting it aside. "That'll do."

"Someone is probably playing a prank," I suggested, giving my own jack-o-lantern the critical eye. It was decidedly lopsided and far more ridiculous than scary.

"It's Cyril. He's haunting me," Lola said firmly.

"Why would he do that?" Cyril had been a rather sweet man. Certainly not the kind of person one expected to go around haunting people.

"He doesn't want me to move on."

I laughed. "That doesn't sound at all like the Cyril I met. He adored you. He'd want you to be happy."

"You didn't know him that well," she said stubbornly.

"Aunt Butty did, and I can assure you she'll agree with me."

"Agree with you about what?" Aunt Butty chose that moment to make her appearance. She was wearing a black caftan embroidered heavily with yellow and orange flowers. She wore a matching turban of orange silk on her head, pinned together with an enormous gold Art Deco pin in the shape of a fan. It was actually rather reserved for her.

"We were speaking about Cyril," I told her. "How much he adored Lola and would want her to move on and be happy."

"Oh, naturally. He'd love nothing more," Aunt Butty said firmly.

"See." I gave Lola a smug look.

She sniffed. Clearly, she wasn't convinced. Or maybe she was just determined to be haunted. Some people are like that, and Lola did love her drama.

Aunt Butty helped herself to tea from the service and sank down into one of the chairs away from the pumpkin disaster. "Now pray tell, what *are* you doing?"

"Carving pumpkins," Lola said. "They say it scares evil spirits away."

Aunt Butty and I exchanged a long look. Maybe we needed more pumpkins.

Chapter 4

The next morning dawned crisp and cold, frost glimmering the grass into crystalline sharp blades and fog hovering low to the ground like a shroud. I gave a delicious shiver. This was perfect Halloween party weather. One could only hope it would hold until the party that evening.

I was grateful to find a fire burning merrily in the dining room grate. Even better, there was a large pot of hot tea steaming away, ready to be poured.

After breakfast, Flora and Maddie quickly cleared the table, then Simon assisted Mr. Singh in piling it high with boxes Aunt Butty had sent down from London. We all gathered 'round to plunder the treasure.

"Lola told me what to get," Aunt Butty said, beaming like Father Christmas. She was wearing a rather startling orange silk velvet dress with an asymmetrical hem and bell sleeves. She'd a brooch in the shape of a black cat pinned to her ample bosom. "Such fun!"

"These are great," Hale said, pulling out a cardboard skeleton that wiggled and jiggled appallingly. "Reminds me of home."

"Ohhh! Fortune telling games," Lola said as she emptied another box. "Swell!"

"What's this?" Chaz held up a cardboard and tissue piece.

"Witch and cauldron." Aunt Butty took it from him. "You see, the cauldron is made of honeycombed tissue paper and it folds out like this." She demonstrated, placing the decoration on the table.

It was indeed a witch, stirring her cauldron while being overlooked by a rather scary owl. There were also mini lanterns meant to cast eerie shadows of ghosts when lit, crepe paper hats in orange with black owls and pumpkins on them, black cats with arched backs, and creepy witches with hooked noses riding brooms. Soon the table was covered in decorations, and Chaz was having a heated debate with Aunt Butty about which should go where.

"Hey, what's the big idea!" Lola held up an envelope.

From where I sat at the other end of the table, I could make out scrawled handwriting, but nothing more. "What is it?"

"A letter of course," she snapped. I noticed there were dark circles under her eyes.

I pursed my lips. "I mean, who is it to? Or from?"

Surprisingly, Lola's hand was a little shaky as she stared at it. "It's to me. From Cyril."

We all stared at her. Finally, Aunt Butty managed, "But that's impossible, dear. Cyril is dead."

"Don'tcha think I know that?" Her gun-moll accent was stronger than ever. "But it's right there in black and white. Look at it if you don't believe me."

Hale, who was closest, took the letter and inspected it. With a shrug, he handed it off to Aunt Butty.

She pulled out her glasses, propped them on her nose, and peered at the writing. "It's certainly Cyril's handwriting. I'd know that indecipherable scrawl anywhere. But what's it doing in my boxes?"

"Good question," Lola said, propping her hands on her hips.

"May I?" At Lola's nod, Mr. Singh plucked the letter from Aunt Butty's hand. "There's no postmark."

Which meant no clue as to when the letter was delivered or by whom. "What about the boxes? When did you pack them, Aunt Butty?"

"I packed them," Mr. Singh said as he handed the letter back to Lola. "The day before we left London. There was no letter inside at that time."

"Says you," Lola snapped.

Mr. Singh gave her an implacable stare. "Yes. I do say."

Lola looked a little faint. Mr. Singh had that effect on people who crossed him.

"Alright, so you packed them. Then what?" I asked.

"They sat on the floor next to the door until the next morning when Simon and I put them in the car," Mr. Singh said. "Once we arrived here, I placed them in the butler's pantry where they stayed until this morning."

"Unlikely anyone would sneak into Aunt Butty's apartment to put a letter in a bunch of Halloween boxes," Chaz muttered. "Not if they valued life and limb."

"Agreed," I said. "An outsider would have had no way of knowing that Aunt Butty had the boxes or that they were coming here where we were meeting Lola. My bet is that someone put the letter into the boxes sometime after they arrived here."

"But why?" Lola wailed. "Is it Cyril? Is he haunting me from the grave?"

Hale snorted, but wisely said nothing.

"Don't be daft, dear," Aunt Butty said. "Why don't you read the letter. Maybe we'll know more then."

This time Lola's hands were definitely shaking as she opened the sealed envelope and pulled out a single sheet of paper. Unfolding it, she read aloud. "My dearest Lola. How I miss you. Don't worry. You'll be with me soon. Love, Cyril." She stared a moment at the letter then let out a shriek. Tossing it toward the fire she dashed from the room screaming, "He's going to kill me!"

Hale managed to grab the letter before the flames could consume it. "Might need this for evidence."

"But of what?" Aunt Butty said. "And how the devil did Cyril send a letter from beyond the grave?"

"You're absolutely certain this is his handwriting?" I pressed.

"I'd stake my life on it."

A shiver went down my spine.

Aunt Butty went off to calm Lola down. Flora followed behind with a tea tray. Personally, I thought it would take more than tea and a few biscuits to calm down the high-strung Lola.

Leaving Chaz and Hale to make sense of the decorations, Mr. Singh showed me the way to the kitchen where Maddie was helping Cook with preparations for the party. The air was hot and close and thick with the scents of cinnamon, vanilla, and oranges.

Cook was a formidable woman who Aunt Butty had picked up along the way somewhere as she did most of her staff. She was nearly as wide as she was tall—testament to her cooking—and had a serious disposition, at least when it came to food. Her face was ruddy from the heat of the fire and her graying hair frizzed out from beneath a cap. Her apron was covered in flour and she'd a smudge of it on her button nose.

"Ladies." With that one word, Mr. Singh drew their attention.

Two pairs of eyes went from Mr. Singh to me and back again. Maddie's gaze held mild curiosity, Cook's annoyance at the interruption.

"Did any of you disturb the boxes which I placed in the butler's pantry?" Mr. Singh gave each one a long look.

"No, sir." It was Maddie who spoke up. "We've been busy you see." She nodded at the piles of biscuits covering the kitchen table. They were all cut into the shapes of pumpkins, witch's hats, or cats.

"Cook, have you seen anything?" I asked.

Cook didn't bother answering, just shook her head and turned back to stir a huge pot of something on the hob. A waft of spicy steam billowed from the pot. She looked not unlike the honeycomb witch and cauldron Chaz had found in one of the boxes.

Just then Flora returned with the empty tea tray. Her eyes grew wide when she caught sight of Mr. Singh. Flora was probably the worst maid in all of Christendom and absolutely everything terrified her, especially the butler. I'd often asked my aunt why she didn't get rid of Flora and hire someone more competent, but Aunt Butty had a soft spot for the girl.

"And you, Flora," I pressed. "Anything?"

The plump young woman shook her head vigorously. "No, miss, not a thing."

"And nothing last night?" Mr. Singh asked.

The three women shook their heads.

"Well, that was a bust," I said as we made our way back upstairs.

"Perhaps." His tone was non-committal.

As we passed along the hall, I caught a glimpse of movement outside one of the windows that opened out into the gardens, as if something dark had flitted by. I turned and caught a shape hovering by the bare lilac bushes. A dark figure in a heavy cowl. When it caught me looking, it turned and disappeared into the overgrown bushes.

"Mr. Singh! There's someone in the garden."

Without grabbing a hat or coat, I dashed down the hall and out the side door and around to the garden. But of the dark figure I'd seen, there was no sign. Only the cold bite of autumn and dead twigs swaying in a slight breeze.

Chapter 5

By the time the guests began to arrive that evening, I'd nearly convinced myself I'd imagined the whole thing. Why ever would someone be lurking in the garden anyhow? When I voiced this thought to Aunt Butty as I helped her zip up her costume—she was dressed as the Queen of Hearts from *Alice's Adventures in Wonderland* complete with an enormous bejeweled crown—she clutched her pearls. Literally.

"It's the ghost," she declared.

"The ghost?" I held back a snicker.

"The ghost of Vessenden Abbey," she said.

"There's no such thing as ghosts, Aunt Butty."

She snorted. "Tell that to the poor monk who wanders the grounds."

"The ghost is a monk?"

"Indeed. You see, there was once a real abbey here on the grounds during the twelfth century. That was before Henry VIII disbanded the monasteries and the building was torn down about four hundred years ago. A few years after that, this house was built and called Vessenden Abbey."

"But what of the ghost?" I pressed.

"They say the grounds are haunted by the ghost of a Benedictine monk who broke his vows of chastity and poverty and now must roam the scene of his debauchery forever." Her voice had taken on a dramatic cast.

"That's utter rot," I insisted.

She shrugged and selected a bright red lipstick to match her gown. "Maybe so, but it does explain what you saw."

It didn't, actually. Not unless I wanted to give in to flights of fancy, but I quickly changed the subject. "There you are. You make a marvelous Queen of Hearts."

"Off with their heads!" she shouted, swinging a gaudy scepter with a sparkly red heart on the end. She eyed me critically. "Is that all you're wearing?"

I glanced down at my gown. It was, I thought, a rather elegant little black number by Mainbocher that had a crisscrossed bodice and a skirt that fell stylishly to the floor with a small train. There was a matching cape that came to mid-thigh and had a fur collar. I'd bought it in Paris, and I didn't get to wear it often enough. "What's wrong with it?"

"Well, it isn't exactly in keeping with the spirit of things, is it? You're meant to wear a costume."

"Oh, well, I've a witch's hat to go with it."

She sighed. "I suppose it will have to do."

"Thank you," I said dryly. "Your approval is what I live for."

"Don't be facetious." She smacked my bottom as if I were a child.

I put on my hat, and we made our way downstairs just as the first of the guests were arriving. The first being, of course, Aunt Butty's dear friend, Louise Pennyfather, and her dog Peaches. Louise wore a black bat costume. The simple black silk crepe dress had enormous bat wings attached which looped around her wrists so that when she held up her arms one could see the bat wings. She wore elbow length black gloves and a black turban on her head with a little toy bat stitched on it. Peaches wore a small pair of bat wings strapped to his back. It was adorable, although Peaches was clearly not thrilled with the whole thing.

"Darling, Butty!" Louise's stentorian tones boomed through the entry. "You've turned the place into a marvel. Such fun!"

The two embraced and I glanced around. Pumpkins with scary faces flickered in the dim light. Thick cobwebs—I had a feeling they were real—festooned every corner and draped thickly about the chandelier. The cardboard articulated skeleton hung in such a way that when the door opened, the breeze sent it dancing a merry jig. It was, in a word, macabre. Fabulously so.

Aunt Butty led the way into the sitting room, which was decorated to the nines with black cats, witches, cauldrons, and more flickering jack-o-lanterns. Hale had taken over the record player and was running through a list of spooky songs from "Dancing the Devil Away" to "The Haunted House" and "Hell's Bells." They were all terribly American and quite fun. Chaz served our chosen cocktail, Dark and Stormy. It was essentially my usual highball only with dark rum instead of whiskey, and for the occasion, he added lychee to look like eyeballs. Ghoulish and adorable at the same time.

At last the proper guests began to arrive, and Mr. Singh—dressed all in black for the occasion—greeted them at the door looking grimmer and more mysterious than usual. He showed each one to the drawing room where he introduced them in what I could have sworn was his attempt at a Transylvanian accent. "Mr. Desmond Bretton and Miss Mary Vaughn."

Desmond Bretton was a rather ordinary looking middle-aged gentleman with a nose that was too large for his face and an overbite that would make my husband's cousin, Bucktooth Binky, look downright handsome in comparison. Mary Vaughn, on the other hand, was young, pretty, and blonde. In fact, her cloud of pale curls reminded me oddly of Lola. Interesting.

Louise, who was standing next to me, leaned over and whispered in a voice that could probably be heard around the entire room, "He's a very successful director. She's an ingénue. Very pretty, don't you think?"

I did. And so, apparently, did Hale. I had to elbow him in the side to get him to shut his mouth.

"I hear," Aunt Butty said in a tone much lower than Louise's, "that she was set to play the lead role. It would have been her breakout. Only the producers wanted someone well known. That's how Lola got the part."

"How'd you hear that?" I asked.

"Flora's aunt works in the costume department," she said.

Of course she did. It was just one of the reasons Aunt Butty kept Flora around, despite her failings as a maid. She had an enormous family with denizens in every career imaginable. She kept my aunt in the best gossip.

"Speaking of Flora, where is she? She was meant to be helping serve drinks." I glanced around, but while Maddie was passing around a plate of gingerbread bats, Flora was nowhere in sight.

"I had to banish her to her room for the evening," Aunt Butty said. "It was that or have Cook quit on me."

"What did the girl do?" Louise boomed, only she pronounced it "gel."

"She upended an entire pot of mulled cider over the kitchen floor, then she broke three plates, shattered a glass vase, and nearly broke Cook's best rolling pin."

"How the devil does a person break a rolling pin?" Chaz asked, handing me a highball glass.

Lychee eyeballs stared blankly at me as they bobbed around in the dark amber liquid. I took a tentative sip. Quite delicious.

"I've no idea," Aunt Butty said, "but if one could do it, Flora could manage. I had to banish her for her own good."

"Not to mention the safety of us all," Hale muttered.

Chaz went to give the newcomers beverages while Mr. Singh announced the next guest. "Miss Trixie d'Vine."

A curvaceous redhead entered the room dressed in a simple witch's costume not unlike my own. Only she made it look beyond fabulous.

Frankly, she needed no introduction. Trixie was the starlet of the moment. Her gorgeous heart-shaped face was everywhere. Her name on everyone's lips. If she was in your film, it sold. Which was why it surprised me Lola had the lead instead of Trixie.

"Miss Nanette Brice," Mr. Singh said solemnly.

Nan Brice was a class act. A famous beauty whose heyday had, if not quite come and gone, was certainly on the wane. She'd been the Trixie of her day. Or maybe the Lola. But while she was aging gracefully, it was obvious she *was* aging. She claimed to be thirty-nine, but I was putting her closer to forty-nine. While not a touch of gray showed in her ink dark hair, her jawline had that hint of softening that comes with age, and tiny crow's feet fanned out from the corners of her eyes. But it was her hands that couldn't hide the truth. The skin was slightly crepey and heavily freckled. Even the glamour of her Cleopatra costume couldn't hide the fact her star was fading.

Aunt Butty bustled over to greet our guests. She welcomed them effusively in true Aunt Butty fashion and ensured everyone was comfortable and had drinks.

"I thought that producer was supposed to be here," Hale murmured.

"Austen Fillmore. Yes, Lola invited him, but he sent his regrets. Some last-minute emergency at the studio," I said.

Louise fed Peaches a bite of gingerbread. He approved.

Mr. Singh cleared his throat, and all our gazes snapped to the door. He straightened his shoulders. "Miss Lola Burns." He stepped back.

There Lola stood in all her glory. Almost quite literally. She wore an incredibly sheer gown held on by bits of gold ribbon. It was meant to be some Greek goddess or other, but she mostly looked like she was running about in her negligee. I hoped she didn't catch her death. The old manor was drafty as anything.

Lola sauntered into the room, stopping in just the right spot to catch the light to best advantage. She threw out her hands in welcome and declared in her best posh voice, "Darlings! So glad you could come!" Unfortunately for her, there was the tiniest hint of gun-moll still lurking below the surface.

Mary snorted back a giggle. Nan merely looked amused. Desmond was all but drooling, and Trixie was more interested in her drink and ogling Hale to pay anyone else any attention.

Lola shot Mary a glare before sashaying over to me. "My darling friend, Ophelia! Have you met everyone?"

I thought she was laying it on a bit thick but played along. "Not as yet, no."

"Come. Let me introduce you." She linked her arm through mine as if we were the best of friends and dragged me over to the Lime Grove people. She reiterated each of their names before finishing off with, "And this is my *dearest* friend, Ophelia, *Lady* Rample."

"Lovely to meet you all," I said in my best lady of the manor voice.

There was a lot of murmuring about how nice it was to meet me and lovely to be here and thanks and all that. I'm not sure anyone was particularly impressed by my title or my posh accent. Or at least not as much as Lola had hoped for. I can only assume that is the reason she blurted out, "Ophelia loves to get herself all twisted up in murder."

The room went dead silent. All eyes were on me. Now usually this isn't a problem, but I admit to being a tad uncomfortable with the attention in this particular instance.

"Lola means Ophelia here *solves* murders," Hale explained, not exactly improving the situation.

"How about a game!" Aunt Butty clapped loudly, drawing everyone's attention away from me. "I'm thinking perhaps charades! Or a rousing game of find-the-skull. It's like hide-and-seek, only one person hides a skull and the rest must find it. Doesn't that sound marvelous?"

Whether or not that sounded marvelous to anyone but Aunt Butty, I was never to discover. The minute the guests' attention was elsewhere, Hale drew me out into the hall.

"How 'bout we take a stroll in the garden?" he said, waggling his eyebrows suggestively.

I grinned. "Let me just get my coat."

In keeping with the theme, I chose a thick, silk velvet jacket in a lovely peach color to throw on over my gown. It wasn't exactly orange, but as orange makes me look bilious, I stay as far away from it as possible. Peach was as close as I would get.

When I rejoined Hale, he had donned his own wool overcoat and fedora. He looked rather smashing. He was the sort of man who could make a pair of ragged overalls look delicious.

Outside, the air held just a hint of the hard bite of winter. My nose was immediately cold, and I wished I was wearing something more substantial on my head than my witch's hat. The moon hung low in the sky, gilding branches with its ghostly glow. I shivered.

"Cold?" Hale drew me closer.

I wasn't about to protest. Instead I snuggled into his warmth, enjoying the scent of spice mixed with smoke and musk that was uniquely him.

Hale tilted my chin up and kissed me sweet and slow. Things were just heating up when movement caught my eye, and I pulled away. He protested.

"Look," I hissed. "That's Lola. What's she doing out here? She'll catch her death."

Sure enough, Lola, dressed in that ridiculous diaphanous gown, came dashing down the walk, her face a rictus of terror. She glanced behind her and that's when I saw the dark shadow hot on her tail, cowl pulled up to hide its face just like the supposed ghost monk I'd seen the previous day.

Lola stumbled and nearly fell, turning around to glance at the monk chasing her. The monk held something up. Lola let out a terrified scream and fainted dead away.

"What the devil?" Hale murmured.

And that's when I saw what the monk was holding: A severed head.

Chapter 6

The severed head dangled in the moonlight, dripping blood onto the paving stones. Drip. Drip. The faceless monk turned toward me, and I swear I felt it to my soul.

"Hey! You, there! Stop!" Hale dashed toward the figure, but the ghostly monk took off running.

"Ghosts don't run," I muttered, hurrying over to wear Lola lay in a heap. I slapped her face gently. "Come on, Lola, get up. You'll catch your death lying here like a ninny." I smacked her a little harder and she groaned. "There you are. Come on now. The bad man is gone." I helped her sit up.

"It wasn't a man," she whispered. "It was a ghost."

"I hardly think so." Although the severed head was rather off-putting.

"It was," she protested. "It's Cyril come to haunt me."

"Cyril was never a monk." At least not that I knew of. I was sure Aunt Butty would have mentioned it.

"M-maybe he sent the m-monk." Whether her teeth were chattering from cold or fright was anyone's guess. In either case, she needed to get warmed up.

"Let's get inside," I urged, hoisting her to her feet. "I'm sure things will look much better when we get some mulled cider into you."

"C-can't," she chattered. "F-Flora spilled it, remember?"

"Oh, dash it all. Why does my aunt keep that girl around? Well, I'm sure we'll find you something. There's got to be brandy somewhere about." Wrapping my arm around her, I hustled her into the house. "Why were you outside?"

"I was using the powder room when I saw something go by the window."

"So you decided to check it out without putting on a coat?" I tutted, completely ignoring the fact I'd done the very same thing earlier.

"What's going on?" Aunt Butty demanded as we entered the sitting room. "We heard a scream."

"Lola had a little run-in with our resident ghost," I informed her as I lowered Lola into the chair closest to the fire. "Chaz, have you got any brandy?"

"Will whiskey do?" he asked, already pouring a healthy dose into a tumbler.

"Ghost?" Nan demanded. "There are ghosts in this house?" She sounded more excited than scared.

"Rumor has it," I admitted as Chaz handed Lola the whiskey.

She downed it in a single gulp and held the glass out for more. As Chaz went for a refill, I glanced around to see if everyone was accounted for. Everyone was. Which meant none of our guests had decided to play ghost. I refused to consider the ghost might actually be real. Utter rot.

Hale returned in a gust of chill air, high color darkening his cheeks, and his breath coming in pants. "He got away."

"You can't catch a ghost," Aunt Butty said stoutly.

"Pretty sure it wasn't a ghost," Hale said, giving Chaz a grateful smile as the latter proffered a glass of whiskey. "Though he did up and disappear."

There was a gasp from the rapt audience.

I rolled my eyes. "What do you mean by 'disappeared'?"

"I mean one minute he was there on the path in front of me, and the next he turned a corner. Only when I turned the same corner... poof! Nobody."

"Impossible," I insisted. "He must have stepped off the path."

Hale shook his head. "Couldn't have. That section is lined on either side by a stone fence. He'd have to be able to walk through walls."

Mary gasped, rather dramatically I thought. "I can't stay here! Not if there are ghosts."

Desmond patted her hand reassuringly. "Now, now. Not to worry, my dear. You're safe with me."

"Ghosts with severed heads," Lola said. "It's Cyril, my husband. I'm telling you he's trying to send me a message!"

Even Aunt Butty went a little pale. "I'd hate to think what sort of message a severed head would be."

"I'm tellin' you," Lola wailed, "he's out to get me!"

Was I the only one with any sense in this house? Before I could say anything scathing, Chaz trod on my foot. I turned to snarl at him, but he held a finger to his lips. For whatever reason, he thought we should go along with it. I shrugged. No skin off my nose.

"How about some mulled wine," Chaz said loudly. "The cider may have been spilled, but Cook managed to whip up a batch. No doubt it's marvelous. Come along to the dining room. We've some nice table games and an enormous spice cake."

As the others filed out of the room, Hale touched my arm. "What is it?"

I shook my head. "It's not Cyril. That's ridiculous."

"Of course it is. There's no such thing as ghosts."

"Not only that," I said, "but Cyril died in America last summer. Don't you think if he was going to haunt her, he'd have done it there?"

He stroked his chin. "Good point."

"Thanks. I thought so."

"If it isn't Cyril haunting her, then who?"

"I don't know," I admitted. "But I'm going to find out."

"Tell me about the notes," I said, sitting on the edge of Lola's bed.

She'd thrown a dressing gown over her costume and was huddled under the covers looking like a half-frozen waif. She blinked, her ridiculously long lashes—I was certain they were fake—fluttering against her cheeks daintily. Her large eyes appeared even larger than usual. "Well, I showed you the one."

"Yes, but I'd like to see it again. And the others. There were others, weren't there?" I was certain of it.

"Yes. But they're stupid. Hand me that bag there." She pointed to a crocodile skin handbag which hung from the wardrobe door.

I collected the bag and handed it to her, returning to my perch. She dumped the contents on the bed: a handkerchief, ticket stub, gold mesh coin purse, compact, two lipsticks, a little sample vial of perfume, and several crumpled envelopes. The latter she handed to me.

The one on top was the letter she'd already shown me. The one she'd found in the Halloween boxes and which Aunt Butty swore was in Cyril's handwriting.

"My dearest Lola. How I miss you. Don't worry. You'll be with me soon. Love, Cyril."

It was such utter nonsense. "This is the most, recent letter, yes?"

"Of course," she snuffled.

"And these others?" I perused them. They all pretty much said the same thing. The first was postmarked a month ago, the very same day Lola had arrived in London. "Did you get any of them while you were in America?"

"No. They all came after I arrived in London. That one was in my hotel room," she said, indicated the first letter. "The others were mostly left in my dressing room or delivered with flowers."

"Delivered?" I inspected those. They had different handwriting and were on cards from a flower shop near Lime Grove Studios. "Did you question the florist?"

"Of course!" she said rather proudly. "I saw how you did it in Hollywood, so I did the same."

"And?" I prodded.

She frowned. "Turns out, they were all anonymous. Cash left in envelopes with instructions for the notes and delivery. No names."

"Hmmm. Interesting." I riffled through the notes again, comparing the ones in Cyril's handwriting. I noticed something odd. His signatures were all the same. I don't mean the same person signed them, but the signatures themselves were identical as if they'd been traced. "Someone forged these. Look." I showed Lola what I'd discovered.

"You sure?" She inspected the signatures, a furrow across her usually smooth brow.

"Positive. No doubt in my mind."

She breathed a sigh of relief. "So what? I got some deranged lunatic after me?"

"Better than a ghost, is it not?"

"I suppose. A lunatic you can catch and throw in the hoosegow."

"The what now?"

She grinned. "The pokey. The clink. The slammer, sister."

"Yes. Jail. Quite. In the meantime, might I keep these?"

"Sure. Why?"

"I'd like to inspect them more thoroughly. Perhaps I might learn something further."

She shrugged. "Do what you like. Me, I'm getting some sleep. I've had enough of this party."

Couldn't say I blamed her.

Chapter 7

Upon further inspection of the letters, I was absolutely convinced the culprit was a woman. I had recently become interested in graphology—the analysis of handwriting—and had read up on the subject. The slant of some of the letters and the slight curl at the ends felt more female than male, and I could have sworn there was the faintest hint of perfume. Something that wasn't Lola's. The question was, what woman would want to terrorize Lola in such a way?

I decided that first I should check out the area where our "ghost" had held up the severed head. I wanted to know for sure if the blood had been real or not, so I collected a

torch from my things—I'd learned to carry one with me—
threw on my coat and headed outside.

It was easy enough to find the spot. Thick drips of
red still dotted the area. Which was odd since blood tended to
try and turn brown. I'd seen enough of it during the Great
War to know that.

The "blood" was sticky and thick to the touch, like
syrup. When I held my fingers to my nose and sniffed, I
caught a whiff of sweet, treacly golden syrup. Definitely fake
blood. How very theatrical.

My best option for learning who might be behind this
whole business was to chat with someone *in* the business, as
it were. And who better to know what was going on behind
the scenes than the director. So I tracked down Desmond
who was hiding out in the library with a pen in one hand and
a Dark and Stormy in the other. When I knocked softly on
the door frame, he glanced up from the notebook he'd been
writing in.

"Oh, Lady, er... Rumple?" He gave what I assumed he
thought was a charming smile, but it made him look more
like a fox in the hen house.

"Rample. Ophelia, please." I sauntered over to take a
seat across from him. "Tired of the party?"

"Well, it got rather odd there, didn't it? Could make for a good film scene, though. Pretty young lady running for her life, being chased by a sadistic killer. Could be a hit."

"I suppose." I didn't mention it wouldn't be to my taste. I preferred my killers safely within the pages of books. Although I did seem to stumble upon them willy-nilly in real life. "I was wondering, Desmond, if you could help me with something."

He closed his notebook. "I could certainly try."

"I was wondering... you know Lola, correct?"

He tilted back in his chair. "As well as any director knows his starlet." As answers go, it was entirely unsatisfying.

"Do you know, would there be someone who had it in for her? Perhaps someone at the studio?"

His eyes widened. "Why do you ask?"

"There have been some... incidents which lead me to believe that someone may be trying to harm her."

"By gosh, that's dreadful. Well, I can't say as she has any enemies. Most people rather like Lola. She's a gas."

"She is that," I agreed. "What about the women here tonight?"

"You think it's a woman?" he asked, astonished.

I gave a noncommittal shrug. "One never knows, does one? The female of the species is more deadly than the male and all that."

His eyes widened. "That's marvelous! Who said that?"

"Kipling, I believe," I said dryly.

He opened his notebook and jotted something down. "Yes, marvelous."

"The women, Mr. Bretton."

"What?" he blinked. "Oh, yes. Well, there were three others up for Lola's role. I suppose that might give them a motive of sorts. You might speak with one of them."

"And which women are they?"

"Why, you already know them. They're all here tonight," he said.

"They are?"

Desmond gave me a strange look. "Yes, of course. Didn't you know? Trixie, Nan, and Mary all wanted the part Lola is playing. In fact, Mary was originally cast as the lead before Lola came along. It likely would have been Mary's breakout role. She was a bit peeved to lose it."

I was betting she was more than peeved. Stardom finally in your grasp only to lose it?

Suddenly I longed for a drink, but I didn't dare leave Desmond alone to go in search of one. I needed to pump him for information, as they say in the American detective novels. "Why *did* Lola come along?"

"The producers wanted a big name." He shrugged. "Lola Burns is a hot commodity right now, and Austen Fillmore worked with Cyril Brumble a time or two."

Interesting. The guest who hadn't shown up had known Cyril. Which would no doubt give Lola a leg up. It also provided another link between the film people and the letters, in a roundabout way. "But isn't Trixie d'Vine one of England's biggest starlets? Surely she would be a big draw."

"Not as big as Lola," he assured me. "There was some discussion of swapping Mary out for Trixie, but I've no idea why it wasn't done."

"You said Nanette Brice was up for the role as well. She's a big name. Why not her?"

He laughed. "The role is a young ingénue torn between her love of the stage and her love for a prince. Nan's a bit long in the tooth for that. She was putting a lot of pressure on Fillmore, but he wouldn't cave. Told her she could play the girl's mother. Should have seen the row."

I bet Nan had loved that. An aging actress who saw her last big chance slipping through her fingers in favor of a brash American. Not to mention the offense at being cast in the role of mother.

I needed to speak to all three women posthaste. All three of them had motive to cause Lola grief. I didn't quite see how they could have pulled it all off, not just yet, but it fit with my feeling that a woman was involved in all of this.

I thanked Desmond and made my way into the sitting room. The fire burned low in the grate, and the record player was still playing something appropriately spooky. Someone had turned off most of the lights so that the room had a wonderfully atmospheric gloom. Mary sat alone, nursing a cocktail and staring out the window into the night.

After helping myself to a cocktail, I took a seat on the sofa beside her. "Quite an evening."

"I suppose." Her eyes didn't leave the black windowpane. "That Lola sure knows how to infuse drama into anything."

"That she does. Where is she?" I knew where Lola was, of course, but I wanted to know if Mary did.

"Gone to bed. Said she was tired."

We sat in silence for a moment. The record came to an end with a scritching sound.

"Desmond told me you were up for the lead role, only Lola got it," I said finally.

"Yes, that's true. It would have been my 'big break,' or so Desmond assures me. I think he's more broken up over it than I am."

"You're not upset about it?" I was admittedly surprised.

"Not at all. I hate making movies," she confided. "It's boring. All that standing about for hours on end doing nothing. Then a flurry of action for a few minutes, only to be told it's all wrong and you must do it again. And again. Until you've done the scene so many times you want to pull your hair out. No, I much prefer the stage. In fact, as soon as this blasted movie is finished, I'm off to the West End to prepare for the true role of a lifetime."

"What's that?" I asked, taking a sip of my drink.

She smiled smugly. "Ophelia in *Hamlet*."

"Goodness. That *is* the role of a lifetime."

"It's going to be marvelous."

"I'm certain it is," I said.

I hadn't realized she was that good an actor. Playing Ophelia on the West End took some real chops. Which led me to wonder, was she acting now? Would I even know if she was?

"Oh, there you are Mary," Trixie said, sauntering into the room. "Desmond is looking for you."

Mary sighed. "Very well." To me she said, "See you later, my lady."

"Ophelia is fine."

"Fancy that." She grinned. "Ophelia and Ophelia." Then she strode out of the room.

"What was that about?" Trixie asked, taking her place.

"She was just telling me about her next role. She seems quite pleased with it."

"Don't let that sweet-as-sugar act fool you," Trixie said. "The kitten has claws. When she wants to. She wasn't at all pleased about getting ousted by Lola, no matter what she says."

I filed that away for further examination later. "What about you?"

"What about me?"

"Desmond says you were up for the ingénue role, too. It must have been vexing to have Lola swan in and take over."

Trixie pursed her lips. "It was. I admit it. I was furious when they gave the role first to Mary, then some outsider. But then I had this fabulous idea."

"What was that?"

"I got a look at the script, and you know who has the best lines?"

"Let me guess. The villain."

Her eyes widened. "Yes! How'd you know?"

"I read a lot." When I wasn't up to my eyeballs in murder and mayhem, of course.

"The villainess… she's just wonderful, you see. So full of fire and passion. So *strong*. Not like these simpering ninnies that are always meant to be the heroines."

"I can see why you'd be drawn to such a role," I said. "You don't strike me as the simpering type."

She burst out laughing. "Nor do you."

"Indeed, I am not. Ask anyone."

We shared a moment of understanding, one woman to another.

"So you tried out for the role of villain," I pressed.

"No, I blackmailed that idiot Desmond to give me the role. He managed to convince the producers. And there you have it. I'm the wicked queen. It's great fun."

"I bet. And you're not upset about losing out on the lead?"

She snorted. "Not even a little. This is far more fun, I'm still getting paid, and you can bet your sweet auntie that a few years from now, no one will remember who played the ingénue, but they'll remember the evil queen."

I'd no doubt she was right.

Unfortunately, that left me right back at square one.

With Trixie crossed off my suspect list, or at least bumped to the bottom, and Mary now without a seeming motive, there was only one woman left to interrogate. Nanette Brice, the fading star.

I knew a little about Nan. She'd had a brief stint on the stage as a teenager before switching to silent films. She'd been in the very first British "talkie" which had solidified her stardom. At least until she passed the forty-year mark and suddenly no one wanted her anymore. The gossip rags were filled with news of her affairs, meltdowns, and financial troubles. I felt rather sorry for her. It was a difficult world for a woman, and I recognized that I was one of the rare lucky ones.

After leaving Trixie in the sitting room, I searched the ground floor thoroughly and found Desmond asleep in the library, glass empty and cigar still smoldering away. I put it out and stuck my head out the French doors to find Hale smoking on the back terrace. Further searching found Chaz chin deep in the liquor cabinet, Mr. Singh trying to placate an irate Mary—apparently her room wasn't to her liking—and Maddie, Flora, and Cook cleaning up the kitchen with help from Simon. What I did not find was Nanette.

Upstairs, I knew precisely where my aunt and Louise were. The latter's booming voice could be heard quite easily drifting from Aunt Butty's room.

"—had to fire him immediately. Can't have that sort of nonsense going on under my roof."

"Indeed not." Aunt Butty's voice was quieter, but still clearly heard through the door.

I padded softly down the hall, not wanting to interrupt, until I came to Nanette's room. I knocked softly, but there was no answer.

"Nan? Are you in there?"

Still no answer.

So I did what any self-respecting nosy parker would do. I turned the brass doorknob. The hinges squeaked ominously. If she'd been asleep, she was awake now.

Except Nanette Brice wasn't asleep. She was lying on her bed, fully dressed, stone cold dead.

Chapter 8

I shrieked for Mr. Singh, knowing he would hear me—the man had the most amazing powers of observation—and dashed across the room, dropping to my knees. I couldn't find a pulse, so I rummaged in her handbag until I found a compact. I held the mirror up under her nose. It fogged faintly. The relief was enough to take the wind out of me.

"My lady?"

"Ring for the doctor, Mr. Singh. She's still alive." I didn't hear his footsteps retreating, but I knew he'd gone.

I didn't know what else to do, so I tucked a blanket around Nanette's still form and then gently slapped her cheeks. No response. That worried me.

"Well, that's the end of that," Desmond said.

I glanced behind me to find him peering around the doorway along with the rest of the household.

"The end of what, pray tell?" Aunt Butty demanded. "The poor woman is dead."

"Precisely," he said rather coldly.

We all stared at him, aghast.

"She isn't dead. She's unconscious," I snapped.

Desmond shrugged. "Too bad. What? You're all thinking it. It's obvious what happened."

"It is?" Lola sounded confused.

"Look around you," Desmond snapped.

We looked.

It was true. The answer was right there in front of us. A monk's cowl was draped across the end of the bed. A Victorian era black gown hung from the wardrobe. Several attempts at letters, all in Cyril Brumble's hand and addressed to Lola, were scattered across the desk. And on the bedside table was an empty bottle of pills.

I crossed the room and picked it up, squinting in the dim light at the small label. "Phenobarbital."

"She took it for sleep," Mary said. When I gave her a look she shrugged. "She told me once she had a hard time sleeping, so the doctor prescribed it."

"She must have taken an overdose," Desmond said. "It's clear she was the person tormenting poor Lola. Probably mad with envy. Lost her head, then couldn't bear to face being caught out so she decided to end it all. Although apparently she failed at even that."

And that seemed to be that. A neat, if sad, wrap up to the whole trying business. Only it didn't sit right with me. It was a little too pat.

After what seemed like forever, the doctor finally arrived. After a quick examination, he had Mr. Singh and Simon carry poor Nan to his vehicle and drove off at top speed for the nearby cottage hospital. No doubt the police would be involved soon enough.

"You believe Desmond's theory?" Hale muttered as we watched the taillights disappear down the drive.

"No, I don't," I admitted. "It's all a little too easy, don't you think?"

"Let's talk about it somewhere we won't be overheard."

Once settled in our room and armed with generous glasses of whiskey, we did just that. Starting with the most obvious.

"Nan couldn't have been the ghost. At least, not on her own."

"Why's that?" Hale took a deep swallow of amber liquid.

"Well, first off, she wasn't even here the night Lola saw the Victorian lady ghost."

"True," he agreed, "they didn't arrive until the next evening. But that doesn't mean she couldn't have snuck into the house somehow and played the part."

"Alright, let's say she did. Somehow, she got into the house and played ghost, but what about the monk? She was definitely not the monk. She was inside with the others at the time."

"Agreed, which means she had to have had someone helping her. Probably a man. The monk was taller than any of the women except maybe Louise."

"I definitely can't imagine Louise playing ghost."

We both grinned at the image.

"I'm still not sure I buy Nan being party to this."

"Why?" he asked.

I stopped to mull it over. "The room... it felt staged."

"What about it felt staged?"

"Everything. The pills... bottle empty, laying on its side next to the glass. Just like in a film. So dramatic." That was it! "It felt like a set."

"If she really wanted to end things, I doubt she'd have worried about putting the cap back on or standing the bottle upright," he pointed out.

"Yes, well, be that as it may, did you notice how the proof of her perfidy was spread out in plain view for all to see? Almost as if it had been laid out by someone who wanted to make sure we got the message that Nanette was involved in haunting Lola. The dress hanging not *in* the wardrobe, but outside where it would be obvious it was a Victorian gown. And then the monk's cowl laid across the bed. She wasn't even the monk, but there it was, the first thing we'd see next to the body. And then the letters. Who writes poison pen letters and then just leaves them out where anyone can find them?" I shook my head. "No, I am convinced it was all staged. It was as if someone was saying, 'Here's the culprit. You don't have to look any further.'"

"It does seem that way," he agreed. "But what about the fact she took those pills?"

"I don't think she did, at least not on purpose. I mean, why would she do it? She had no reason to," I pointed out. "Nobody had any clue she was involved. I wanted to speak to her as a possible perpetrator, but there was nothing solid, no real evidence to point in her direction. She'd have had no way of knowing I had any intention of questioning her. And even if she did, she was an excellent actress. She could have easily played innocent, and I doubt I could have proved otherwise. Well, I probably could have, but it would have been difficult."

"Do you think she was involved in the scheme at all?"

"That I'm not sure. If she was, she had help. And if she had help... No, I don't believe she overdosed on purpose. Or even at all. I am convinced it was attempted murder, and by either her partner, or the real perpetrators."

It was only ten o'clock, still early by London standards, so we made our way back downstairs for more cocktails and possibly another piece of cake. I was also hoping to find out more about the Lime Grove people.

Hale joined Chaz and Desmond for a round of billiards, and I found Trixie and Mary mixing drinks in the sitting room. They looked up when I entered.

"Try this," Trixie said. "We call it the Nanette. In her honor."

"She's not dead," I reminded them.

"Of course not," Mary said. "But she *is* an icon. She should have her own cocktail, don't you think?"

"I suppose you're right. What's in it?" I tasted it. It was overly sweet and a little fruity. Not at all like Nanette Brice.

Trixie frowned. "You know, I have no idea. I think rum, whiskey, some of whatever this green stuff is, plus some fruit juice Mr. Singh dug up."

"I think perhaps it needs a little work," I suggested.

Mary took a swallow. "She's right. I'm going down to the kitchen to see if I can sneak some of that mulled whatever Cook was making. I bet that would be good mixed with... something."

Trixie shook her head. "I don't think either one of us should be mixing cocktails. Clearly we haven't the gift for it."

I made a non-committal sound. "Aren't you worried about Nan?"

"Worried is too strong a word, but I do hope she pulls through. She's a good egg." Trixie eyed me. "Do you think she was behind all this ghost business and messing about with Lola's head?"

"Do you?" I countered.

She left her half-finished drink on the sideboard and sat down, one foot tucked under her. "I wouldn't have thought so. She doesn't seem the type to resort to it, but you never know about people, do you? She must have been desperate. She should have gone to Fillmore."

"Austen Fillmore? The producer?"

"Sure. They used to have a thing. If she begged him hard enough, I bet he'd have done something, but she wouldn't. She's a proud one, our Nan."

"Why didn't Fillmore come tonight? Lola said she invited him."

She lifted a shoulder. "No idea. Busy, I suppose."

I filed that away for later. "If Nan was behind the ghost business, she would have had to have help."

She nodded slowly. "Yes, I can see that. Perhaps someone with a background in makeup and special effects. Someone who could pull off the ghost gag."

I lifted a brow. It made sense. The severed head with all that blood came to mind. "Any idea who that could be?"

"Only one person I can think of."

"Who?" I sat up straighter.

"He used to be a props manager and he was a whiz at special effects before he became a director," she said. "Desmond. Desmond could have done it."

Shéa MacLeod

Chapter 9

After making my excuses to Trixie, I took a quick walk through the garden to inspect the wall where Hale said the ghost disappeared. Once I satisfied my curiosity, I'd a quick word with my aunt and Lola, then made my way into the billiards room. The gentlemen were still playing, the room thick and blue with smoke.

"I think we have it solved," I announced.

Three pairs of eyes focused on me.

"What solved?" Chaz asked.

"Why the ghost business, of course. And the letters." I picked up one of the balls, inspected it, and put it back down.

"And?" Hale prompted, hiding a smile behind his cigar.

"Lola says she has proof of who the real ghost is. And it isn't Nanette Brice." I paused in triumph.

Desmond let out a guffaw. "Lola is crazy. Can't trust a word that dame says."

"I assure you, that is not the case." My tone was a tad tart. I was getting tired of his superior attitude. "She has proof. I've seen it with my eyes. She knows who tried to kill Nan."

"Who was it?" Chaz demanded.

"Yes," Desmond said, eyes narrowing. "Who was it?"

"I don't know," I admitted. "She wouldn't tell me."

Desmond stormed toward the door. "Then she needs to tell us straight away."

We trailed him up the stairs where he banged viciously on Lola's door. There was no answer.

"What's the plan?" Chaz muttered.

"I thought I knew, but this wasn't part of it," I admitted, suddenly nervous. Why wasn't Lola answering?

Desmond rattled the knob. "It's locked."

"Lola! Are you in there?" I shouted through the door.

"What is going on out here?" Louise's voice boomed through the hall. "A person can't even think with all this noise." At her side, Peaches let out an irritated woof.

"Where's Lola?" my aunt demanded.

"What's happening?"

"What's the racket?"

Various voices chimed in as everyone drifted in from wherever they'd been. None of them was Lola.

"We need to get this door open," I said.

"Stand back." Mr. Singh appeared out of nowhere, a poker in his hand. He hit the knob smartly and it clattered to the floor.

"Jolly good, old man," Desmond shouted, thrusting open the door.

The room beyond was empty save for a jumble of clothing strewn about, and the scent of perfume fresh in the air. No Lola.

"Where's she got to?" Aunt Butty demanded.

"I don't know," I admitted. "But we need to find her. Quickly."

We all dashed about the house madly, crisscrossing the halls, shouting for Lola and occasionally running into each other. Chaz checked the attic and Mr. Singh the wine cellar. Simon made a thorough search of the garage, while Maddie investigated the long empty stables with Hale by her side. Cook made quick work of the servants' quarters alone since no one could find Flora either. The rest of us divvied up the remaining rooms, searching them thoroughly.

"Not a sign of her," Aunt Butty said. Her crown was askew, gray curls festooned with cobwebs, and there was a smudge of dust along one plump cheek.

"Where could that girl have got to?" Louise demanded of no one in particular.

"This can't be good," Trixie muttered.

Mary threw her a look. "What do you know about it?"

"Listen you little nitwit—"

"Ladies!" I threw up my hands. "Any other ideas where Lola could have got to?"

"Perhaps she just took off," Mary suggested. "Got tired of this whole thing."

"In the middle of her party?" Aunt Butty shook her head. "I don't think so. Louise was just about to get out her cards. Lola can never resist the cards."

Louise was a proponent of spiritualism, though it was no longer in fashion. Tarot cards were her specialty.

"How do you know Lola likes the tarot?" I demanded.

"She told me," Aunt Butty said. "Or rather, she told Louise when Louise mentioned it."

"There is an alarming amount of people going missing," I said. "First Lola. Now Flora."

"Flora probably fell asleep somewhere," Aunt Butty said. "You know what she's like."

"Bloody useless," Louise boomed.

"Now, Louise, the girl does her best," Aunt Butty protested.

"Surely we'd have found her while we were searching," I pointed out.

"We didn't find Lola," Trixie said. "Maybe the two of them are together."

"Maybe there's a secret passage or a hidden room or something," Mary said with wide eyes.

"Good idea," Chaz said as he entered the room with Hale, Desmond, and Mr. Singh. "A lot of these old houses had priest holes and such. Question is, how are we going to find it if there is one?"

"Did anyone check the gatehouse?" Desmond asked. "It looked like it had been abandoned for years. Good place to hide someone."

We all grabbed Halloween lanterns—as that was what was closest to hand—and charged down the drive toward the gatehouse. If anyone would have been watching, no doubt we'd have looked quite the sight dashing about in our garish costumes with flickering yellow and orange lanterns casting eerie shadows of cats and pumpkins.

The gatehouse loomed a dark hulk in the night. The wind moaned as it circled around the eaves, and an owl hooted nearby. It would have been deliciously creepy if I wasn't so worried about Lola.

The door was locked tight, but in the dim light of the lanterns, it was clear it had been opened recently. A wide bare patch shown through the thick carpet of decaying leaves.

"This is it," I said. "I'm sure of it. Lola!"

We all listened. There was a muffled sound from inside like a cat mewling or a baby crying.

"Mr. Singh, break down the door!" Aunt Butty ordered dramatically.

It only took a couple thrusts of his broad shoulder to smash the door down. We all tumbled inside. There, in the center of the dusty, dank room, tied to a chair, sat Lola. Black streaks of mascara dripped down her cheeks, her hair was a tousled mess, and whoever had taken her had used a pair of silk stockings to gag her.

While Chaz and Mr. Singh went to work untying her hands and feet, I undid her gag. The minute she was free, she lurched from her chair and threw her arms around my neck, nearly choking me to death.

"Ophelia, thank God you came!"

"What happened?" I asked, just barely managing to keep her from choking me to death.

Her eyes were wide. "It was the monk! The ghost monk. He took me prisoner. Dragged me first to some room in the manor, and then later out here."

"It couldn't have been a ghost, Lola," I said a little tartly. "Ghosts don't tie people up."

"Well, this one did," she said stubbornly.

"Did he say anything?" Trixie asked.

Lola shook her head, her blonde curls bouncing. Despite her ordeal, she was as beautiful as ever. "Oh, no. He didn't say a thing."

"Then how do you know it was a he?" Hale pointed out.

She frowned. "Well, he smelled like a man. Cigar smoke and bay rum."

I admittedly knew of no women who used bay rum in scent. It was usually found in men's shaving soaps. Hale used a cream from America called Colgate that had a sort of fresh smell to it. Chaz used something with sandalwood. And Mr. Singh didn't shave, letting his beard grow luxurious and thick. The only man here who smelled of bay rum was—

"You mean, like Desmond," I said softly.

She blinked baby doll eyes. "Yes. Exactly like Desmond."

"That's nonsense!" Desmond sputtered.

"Is it?" I shot him a glare. "Makes perfect sense to me. It was you who played ghost. You who sent Lola those letters."

"Why would I do that?" he scoffed. "That's bananas."

"I don't know," Trixie drawled. "Makes a strange sort of sense to me. You've had a thing for Lola since before she arrived."

"And you a married man." Mary shook her head as if she'd never heard of such a thing.

"Ridiculous nonsense!" Desmond snarled.

"You have a thing for little ole me?" Lola fluttered her lashes.

Desmond blushed furiously. His mouth opened and closed but nothing came out. Finally, he said, "I wasn't the ghost. I couldn't have been. I was in the sitting room with all of you. And Mr. Davis here said the ghost disappeared in the middle of a stone wall."

"A wall with a door in it." I reveled in my little reveal. "I went exploring earlier and found the door hidden under a bunch of ivy. It leads right to the veranda outside the sitting room. You could have easily slipped in and out with no one the wiser."

He spluttered a bit.

"Here's what I think happened," I said. "You were in love with Lola and Nan found out. It was her only leverage and she was willing to use it ruthlessly. She threatened to tell your wife unless you helped her, so you agreed to plague Lola with notes and gifts from her dead husband. Nan thought it would drive Lola crazy, forcing her out of the film. And it came close."

"Did not," Lola muttered.

We ignored her. "When she didn't drop out of the movie, you used the party to play ghost. Maybe you thought that when Lola had a meltdown you could sweep in and play shining knight. But Lola didn't have a breakdown, and Nan was losing her patience. You couldn't have her blabbing on you, so you tried to kill her and made sure all the evidence against her was there front and center so there'd be no question who was behind it all. Except it didn't quite work. And then I told you Lola knew who the attempted killer was, so you had to shut her up."

"Rubbish!" Desmond shouted. "Lola obviously went missing *before* you told me she knew who the killer was. I couldn't have taken her. I was with you the whole damn time. And before that, I was with Chaz and Hale. I never touched Lola!"

"Oh." I blinked, then mentally called myself seven kinds of idiot. "Of course. Of course not. It couldn't be you."

"That's what I'm saying!" he bellowed.

"Come on now," Aunt Butty urged. "It's cold out here. Let's all go into the house and warm up."

We were nearly to the house when it dawned on me. "Fillmore."

"But Fillmore isn't here," Trixie said.

"Exactly. Fillmore isn't here. He was the perfect patsy. Easily blamed and unable to defend himself. Which was why the attempted murderer convinced him to skip the party."

"Must we do this in the cold and dark?" Aunt Butty moaned, despite the fact we stood in a pool of light spilling from the sitting room, and it was chilly but not terribly cold.

I ignored her, turning to glare at Desmond. "I was right about everything. You and Nan. Her blackmailing you. Her being behind the attempts to drive Lola crazy. But I wasn't right about one thing. It wasn't you who drugged Nan. She would have never let you close enough for that. She's not a stupid woman. She wouldn't give you the opportunity. And it wasn't you who took Lola because, as you pointed out, you have an alibi and you had no idea we were setting a trap for you. No, there was one other person. One with a motive I didn't see."

"Who?" Trixie demanded.

"You." I pointed at Mary.

Mary's eyes widened in an approximation of Lola's earlier. Her mouth made a little oh shape. "Me? Don't be daft."

"Yes, you. You knew all about Nan's little game. Knew from the beginning. And you were fine with it because you hoped that it would get rid of Lola, leaving the way open for you to take Lola's part. You knew they'd never give it to Nan. She was too old and didn't have enough draw at the box office. No, no matter what she believed, her days were over, and you knew it."

"I told you, I don't care about the part," she said. "I'm focusing on the stage."

"Maybe," I admitted. "Perhaps it's true you prefer the stage, but there's a little problem. You are in love with Desmond."

Desmond gaped.

Trixie laughed.

Mary blinked. "No, I'm not."

Trixie laughed harder. "Of course, you are. You've been mooning over him since the day you arrived on set."

Mary's cheeks reddened unattractively. "This is ridiculous."

"Not really. Desmond is handsome for a man of his age," I said. Which was an out-and-out lie, but there's no accounting for taste.

"Gee, thanks," Desmond muttered.

Ignoring him, I went on, "He's talented. Well off. Connected. You figured if you could get your claws in him, he would be good for your career. When Nan started causing problems, you figured you could use this weekend as your golden opportunity to solve his problem for him. That would really sink your claws in. First, you convinced Fillmore to skip the party. No doubt you told him it would look bad for his image or something. You figured you could point the finger at him once everyone figured out Nan had a male coconspirator. Then you slipped into her room and tried to poison her, making sure all the evidence was out where everyone could see it."

"Couldn't have." Mary crossed her arms. "I was with you when Nan took those pills."

"Poison can be administered at any time," I said. "Besides, you left. You had plenty of time."

"Wait!" Aunt Butty held up her hands. "How did she make sure Nan took the poison? You can't force pills down a person's throat."

"Except that Mary is the one who told us Nan took sleeping pills. No one else knew that." I glared at Mary.

"You saw the bottle in her room," she snapped.

"That bottle could have belonged to anyone," I pointed out. "In fact, it could have just as easily belonged to you. You placed it there as a prop. The real dose came earlier, no doubt in liquid form added to her cocktail. That's why she went to bed early. She was already feeling the effects."

"If you say so," Mary said with an eye roll.

"Only your plan didn't quite work," I continued, "so you had to come up with something else. You were next door when I was talking to Lola about our plan to lay a trap for Desmond, and you knew and you didn't want him to expose his part in the ghost plan, so you're the one who kidnapped Lola, first stashing her somewhere in the manor, then when we were searching for her, you moved her to the gatehouse."

"How did I do that?" Mary sneered. "Even she said the kidnapper was a man."

"Because of the bay rum!" Lola declared.

"Which was already on the monk's cowl because Desmond was wearing it the night he chased Lola through the garden. That's what you smelled," I told her.

"That makes sense," Lola agreed.

"You tried to kill Nan and Lola because of a man?" Trixie turned to Mary. "What a nitwit. You do realize you've ruined your life. You'll go to jail for this."

"No doubt they all will," I said dryly.

"They'll have to catch me first!" Mary declared. And she took off running.

Trixie rolled her eyes. "So dramatic."

Chaz started after her, but Mr. Singh held him back. He picked up one of the small, hand-size pumpkins we'd set out for decoration, hefted it, and let fly. It smacked into Mary's back and sent her sprawling face-first into the mud. She let out an unladylike howl.

"I'll go ring the police, shall I?" Without waiting for an answer, Mr. Singh made his way into the house.

Hale shook his head. "That man coulda been in the majors."

I was just glad he was on our side.

Chapter 10

It was the small hours of the morning before the police finally arrived to cart off Mary and Desmond for questioning. We'd also been informed that Nanette had survived and was awake and would be charged for her part in harassing Lola.

"No doubt the courts will go easy on her seeing as how she was nearly killed," Chaz mused.

"Not to mention she's famous," Lola said.

We lounged around the sitting room fire, watching the sun come up. Cook had provided us with coffees liberally dosed with whiskey, cream, and honey. Aunt Butty and Louise had changed into their dressing gowns but had made no attempt to reach their beds. Peaches was curled up at Louise's feet, still dressed like a bat. The rest of us had swapped our costumes for more comfortable—and warm— clothing, but no one seemed eager to sleep.

"If I were a betting woman, I'd say she's going to come up smelling of roses," Louise said.

"You got that right," Lola agreed. She looked rather adorable in men's style flannel pajamas.

"What do you mean?" Aunt Butty asked.

"It's real simple, Auntie," Lola said. "There's a saying in Hollywood. All publicity is good publicity. Especially if it's free. Somethin' you swells ain't figured out yet. You can bet your bottom dollar that Nanette is gonna be back on her feet in no time."

Aunt Butty and Louise exchanged bemused glances. They were definitely from an era where publicity was never considered a good thing, but I understood what Lola meant. In the world of showbiz, if your name was out there in front of the people, you were winning, no matter how it got there.

"Are you feeling better now, Lola?" I asked.

"Sure thing, ducks. I knew it couldn't be Cyril, what with him being dead and all." She tossed back the dregs of her coffee. "Ghosts ain't real."

I didn't bother pointing out she'd been quite convinced it *had* been Cyril and that she'd absolutely believed ghosts were real. Maybe rewriting history was the best thing for her mental state.

Hale touched my shoulder. "It's been a long day and an even longer night. We should get some rest."

"I couldn't sleep—"

"AEEEEAH!" Louise let out a bloodcurdling scream, joined shortly by Lola and Trixie.

"What the deuce!" Chaz shouted, nearly dropping his cup.

For there in the doorway, half hidden by shadows, was a ghostly woman dressed in a white Victorian gown. The ghost shrieked.

Louise shrieked louder.

Aunt Butty started laughing. And that's when I realized the "ghost" was actually Flora dressed up, her face and hair covered in white powder.

"Flora! What is going on?" I demanded.

"S-sorry, M-miss, but L-lady B-Butty asked me to."

Aunt Butty laughed harder. So hard she couldn't get any words out.

"It's 'my lady,' Flora, and what did my aunt ask you to do?" I said tartly. "Spit it out."

"Sh-she told me I ought to be a ghost. I was meant to hide in the morning room and come in and s-scare everyone at the party for a laugh and all, only I fell asleep while I was waiting."

"The morning room where Mary was supposed to search. No wonder no one found her," I said.

"And I forgot," Aunt Butty admitted. "All the confusion...it just flew right out of my head."

No surprise there.

Flora looked around in confusion. "Sorry I was late. Did everyone leave?"

I don't think I'd ever laughed so hard in my life.

The End.

Coming Soon
Lady Rample Mysteries
Book Nine

Sign up for updates on Lady Rample:
https://www.subscribepage.com/cozymystery

Note from the Author

Thank you for reading. If you enjoyed this book, I'd appreciate it if you'd help others find it so they can enjoy it too.

Lend it: This e-book is lending-enabled, so feel free to share it with your friends, readers' groups, and discussion boards.

Review it: Let other potential readers know what you liked or didn't like about the story.

Sign Up: Join in on the fun on Shéa's email list: https://www.subscribepage.com/cozymystery
Book updates can be found at www.sheamacleod.com

About Shéa MacLeod

Shéa MacLeod is the author of the bestselling paranormal series, Sunwalker Saga, as well as the award nominated cozy mystery series Viola Roberts Cozy Mysteries. She has dreamed of writing novels since before she could hold a crayon. She totally blames her mother.

She resides in the leafy green hills outside Portland, Oregon where she indulges in her fondness for strong coffee, Ancient Aliens reruns, lemon curd, and dragons. She can usually be found at her desk dreaming of ways to kill people (or vampires). Fictionally speaking, of course.

Shéa MacLeod

Other books by Shéa MacLeod

Lady Rample Mysteries
Lady Rample Steps Out
Lady Rample Spies a Clue
Lady Rample and the Silver Screen
Lady Rample Sits In
Lady Rample and the Ghost of Christmas Past
Lady Rample and Cupid's Kiss
Lady Rample and the Mysterious Mr. Singh
Lady Rample and the Haunted Manor

Sugar Martin Vintage Cozy Mysteries
A Death in Devon
A Grave Gala

Viola Roberts Cozy Mysteries
The Corpse in the Cabana
The Stiff in the Study
The Poison in the Pudding
The Body in the Bathtub
The Venom in the Valentine
The Remains in the Rectory
The Death in the Drink

Deepwood Witches Mysteries
Potions, Poisons, and Peril
Wisteria, Witchery, and Woe
Magic, Moonlight, and Murder (Coming Soon)

Intergalactic Investigations
Infinite Justice
A Rage of Angels

Notting Hill Diaries

Kissing Frogs
Kiss Me, Chloe
Kiss Me, Stupid
Kissing Mr. Darcy
Cupcake Goddess Novelettes
Be Careful What You Wish For
Nothing Tastes As Good
Soulfully Sweet
A Stich in Time

Dragon Wars
Dragon Warrior
Dragon Lord
Dragon Goddess
Green Witch
Dragon Corps
Dragon Mage
Dragon's Angel
Dragon Wars- Three Complete Novels Boxed Set
Dragon Wars 2 – Three Complete Novels Boxed Set

Sunwalker Saga
Kissed by Darkness
Kissed by Fire
Kissed by Smoke
Kissed by Moonlight
Kissed by Ice
Kissed by Blood
Kissed by Destiny

Sunwalker Saga: Soulshifter Trilogy
Fearless
Haunted
Soulshifter

Made in the USA
Coppell, TX
15 November 2020

41389532R00059